Lavender

Lavender Blue

& the Faeries of Galtee Wood

Written by

Steve Richardson

Illustrated by

Larry MacDougall

Foreword by

Michael Wm. Kaluta

Book Design by

Thomas Haller Buchanan

Impossible Dreams PUBLISHING CO.

Dedication

Lavender Blue and the Faeries of Galtee Wood was written
in loving memory of three children, my brother John and
nephews Kendall and Evan who now live somewhere on
another world a million miles beyond the clouds. Each time
a child passed on, the family witnessed the sight of a majestic
rainbow shimmering like a beacon of hope in a dark stormy
sky. I have come to believe when the human spirit flies free
constantly reaching for the stars and striving to soar aloft —
always believing in love, goodness and magic — the future is
limited only to what the human imagination can dream!

I firmly believe in chasing rainbows and I firmly believe the
world of tomorrow can be a world of peace and love for all.
The answers to every problem lie in the hearts of all
humanity and are hidden inside the abstract framework of
the universe waiting to be released by anyone with a steadfast
belief that nothing is impossible with love and hope!

Steve Richardson

—2013

Library of Congress Cataloging-in-Publication Number: 2012922088

ISBN 0-9786422-4-4

Cover illustration by Larry MacDougall

Cover and Book Design by Thomas Haller Buchanan

Published by Impossible Dreams Publishing
4123 Rancho Grande Pl. NW
Albuquerque, NM 87120

Visit us on the web!

www.impossibledreamspub.com

FOREWORD

Here's an eternal story dressed up for the Faerie Ball. Once read, the story will have always existed, and, though magically specific, is a story each reader will make their own. Lavender Blue and the Faeries of Galtee Wood is a tale in which to become lost, to wander, to wonder, to find yourself again in reflection, wide eyed and smiling into your open heart... it awakens ancestors' dreams in the young while reawakening those older readers who had set their dreams aside as Real Life bustled them into adulthood.

Larry MacDougall's art brightens sunlight into the haunted woods, brings moonlight underground and charms a song from the air between the shadowed branches. From cover to cover, Lavender Blue embodies what books have always kept in trust: a place to take yourself where "away" always feels like "home"... a moment that closes quietly only to open once more in the mind's eye.

Herein is heroism born of need, and who wouldn't say there's nothing that one needs more than Courage.

> *"Courage is the price that Life exacts for granting peace.*
> *The soul that knows it not*
> *Knows no release from little things:*
> *Knows not the livid loneliness of fear,*
> *Nor mountain heights where bitter joy can hear*
> *The sound of wings.*
>
> *How can life grant us boon of living, compensate*
> *For dull gray ugliness and pregnant hate*
> *Unless we dare The soul's dominion?*
> *Each time we make a choice, we pay*
> *With courage to behold the restless day,*
> *And count it fair."*
>   —*Amelia Earhart*

   —Michael Wm. Kaluta, New York, NY

Michael is a world-renowned book illustrator and comic book artist, a modern legend for his classic work.
Among other honors, he received the 2003 Spectrum Grandmaster Award and was inducted into the
Will Eisner Award Hall of Fame amongst all the greats of the entire history of comics.

My wish for you:

I wish you not a path devoid of clouds, nor a life on a bed of roses,
Not that you might never need regret,
Nor that you should never feel pain.
No, that is not my wish for you.
My wish for you is:
That you might be brave in times of trial,
When others lay crosses upon your shoulders.
When mountains must be climbed and chasms are to be crossed,
When hope can scarce shine through.
That every gift God gave you might grow with you
And let you give your gift of joy to all who care for you.
That you may always have a friend who is worth that name,
Whom you can trust and who helps you in times of sadness,
Who will defy the storms of daily life at your side.

— Anonymous Irish blessing

Chapter **1**

In a cottage at the edge of the mysterious Galtee Woods lived a girl named Lavender Blue O'Malley.

She was named after the lavender flower, and because she was born on a day when the sky was blue and the sun shone down upon the vale, her middle name was Blue.

On a sunny spring day, Lavender was most often found out in the garden with her best friend Rose, trying to catch butterflies, or exploring in the dark woods behind the house looking for frogs and salamanders in the brooks and lily ponds. However, sunny days were rare, and she and Rose were often forced inside to play games or read.

This particular day, which was sunny but with clouds approaching, she was by herself in the garden, cutting flowers to take to her friend. Rose had become very ill and could not leave her bed.

"I hope Rose will like these," Lavender thought. "Maybe they will remind her of all the times we use to pick flowers and leave them on Mrs. Dougall's doorstep, then knock on the door and run and hide!"

This had been Rose's favorite game, because Mrs. Dougall was widowed and lived all alone. Rose especially liked seeing Mrs. Dougall's pleasant yet baffled reaction to the mysterious flowers.

"I am sure those old stories will make her laugh. She loves to make people feel happy," thought Lavender.

As she clipped each flower with great care, placing them into her basket, a concerned look came over her face. "Rose looked to be in so much pain the last time I was there, so thin and looking worse with each visit. I do hope she looks better this time. We haven't been able to play together for weeks."

With cut roses in her basket, Lavender walked through the countryside to Rose's cottage. When she arrived, Rose was sleeping and her mother was watching over her. Lavender handed the roses to Mrs. O'Brien, who arranged them in a vase next to Rose's bed. As they stood together watching Rose sleep, Mrs. O'Brien put her arm around Lavender's shoulder.

"She had a difficult night, Lavender" said Mrs. O'Brien, looking down sadly upon her daughter. "You should know she has very little time left. I fear the Banshee's cry could come any night."

Lavender's mouth dropped open. "But Mum says the Banshee only comes and cries when someone is going to die!" Tears began to well up in her eyes. "You're wrong, Mrs. O'Brien, she will get better, I know she will! She has to! She is too nice a person for God to take. She is the best friend anyone could ever wish for, and she never thinks about herself. She is my very best friend. God can't take her now!"

Lavender wiped more tears away and sniffled several times, trying to hold back the tears. Then she laid her hand on Rose's hand. A few minutes later, Rose began to wake up, and a small smile came upon her face when she saw Lavender and felt the gentle touch of Lavender's hand. Though very weak, Rose shifted to face her friend.

"It's wonderful to see you, Lavender. I hope you can stay a while." Rose turned to look out the window. "Looks like another rainy day." Then she began to cough, and her breathing grew wheezy and weak.

Lavender noticed how pale and thin Rose looked, and how her eyes could hardly stay open. It was clear Rose was much worse than during her last visit. Lavender tried to seem cheerful for Rose. She smiled, wiping away the last tears.

"Yes, it's raining but the sun will come out soon, just you wait and see. It was out this morning! I bet we will see a rainbow before the day is through. You will be better in no time, Rose, and before you know it we will be playing in the woods and putting flowers on Mrs. Dougall's doorstep."

A sad look overtook Rose's face. Lavender could see her friend was giving up. "Look, Rose, I even picked you some roses to remind you of Mrs. Dougall."

Rose smiled just a little and struggled to speak. "Can you hold the flowers next to my face? I want to smell them. Poor Mrs. Dougall, such a sweet, lonely woman."

Lavender put the flowers next to Rose's nose. Rose attempted to smell them but then began to cough again, this time worse than before. She coughed for several seconds, then her eyes closed and she fell back to sleep.

More tears began running down Lavender's cheeks. She could hardly believe that her very dearest friend might soon be gone. She wanted to stay until Rose woke up again, but Mrs. O'Brien thought it best if Rose rested and didn't try to talk. Sadly, Lavender headed home for the evening, having seen Rose for only a few brief minutes.

As Lavender walked through the countryside, so pretty in the light rain, powerful fears about losing Rose continued to well up from deep inside her. She couldn't bear the idea that Rose would not be around to play on these misty green hills covered in clover and grass. Lavender felt helpless, she so desperately wanted to help Rose get better.

As she neared home, darkness overtook the woods around her. The piercing cry of an owl in the distance sent shivers up Lavender's spine. Her thoughts instantly turned toward the Banshee, the mournful faerie woman who brings the message of death. What if the Banshee was somewhere out there, and knew just when Rose was to die? Lavender quickened her pace, and a resolve formed in her that if she did see the Banshee, she would do everything in her power to keep the faerie away from Rose's house.

That night while Lavender was getting undressed for bed, something fell from her clothes to the floor. She picked it up and to her surprise found a broken-off rosebud from the flowers she had picked for Rose. It had not opened yet but was still very beautiful. As she held it, a thorn pricked her finger, which began to bleed.

"Ouch!" said Lavender. "I will keep this rosebud forever to remind me of my dear friend Rose and how deeply I love her. I don't ever want to forget her." Lavender crawled into bed and blew out the lamp next to her. She was still holding the rosebud in her hand. "Tomorrow I will pick some lavender flowers and put them in a box with this rosebud to remind me of our friendship."

Lavender rolled over, facing the open window by her bed. She could smell the cool damp air softly blowing on her face. Pushing the lace curtains back, she saw the stars sparkling over the forested hills. She held the rosebud tightly, though careful of the thorn, thinking of her dear friend as she gazed at the stars.

She said a little prayer out loud: "I would do anything to save Rose, anything at all. Please let me have that chance, please, God, even if that means taking me instead of Rose!"

Just then, a falling star flashed purple across the sky. Lavender felt almost as if someone had been listening and was sending her a sign. A peaceful feeling come over her, a feeling that maybe everything would be all right, or at least that Rose would be taken care of in Heaven. Lavender fell fast asleep, still holding the rosebud in her hand.

As she slept, the moon rose over the hills, casting light onto her face. The hands on the clock slowly moved round to midnight. Then, far off in the distance, a tiny star began moving toward Lavender's window. The light grew brighter and closer, until a forest pixie landed right on the windowsill and slid into Lavender's room. It gracefully jumped onto Lavender's shoulder, and then pulled the covers back to see Lavender's hand and the rosebud.

The little faerie glowed faintly, lighting up Lavender's face. It waved its hand, and the rosebud became a thousand golden sparkles, then changed into a silver necklace with a charm attached, shimmering faintly from the glow of the little forest creature. The faerie gently closed Lavender's hand and kissed her on the cheek. Then it jumped to the windowsill and flew across the starlit sky, disappearing into the dark Galtee Woods.

Chapter 2

When Lavender awoke in the morning, she instantly remembered the falling star, and a spark of hope went through her.

The sun was shining, and she could smell the flowers outside her room and hear the birds singing up a storm.

"What a perfect day!" she thought, but the happy feeling disappeared the moment she remembered Rose lying sick in her bed. "I hope Rose is awake and well enough to look outside and see how beautiful it is."

Lavender opened her hand and saw that the rosebud was gone. Instead, she was holding a beautiful silver necklace and charm! The chain was very intricate, and the charm was a silver circle with a line across the middle, a silver arrow going into it and a golden arrow going out.

"How did this get into my hand?" Lavender wondered. "Perhaps Mum and Dad put this here and took the rosebud?" She looked under the covers and under the bed and in every possible place the rosebud might have ended up, but found nothing.

Lavender held up the necklace to look at it closely. "Such a curious symbol, especially the golden arrow. I must ask Mum and Dad if they know what this could mean."

At breakfast, Lavender told her parents about the rosebud and the necklace. At first they didn't believe her, but when she showed them the necklace, they were just as amazed as she was. They had no idea where the necklace had come from or what the charm meant.

Lavender's mother began to clear the table. "Perhaps you can ask Professor Priddle at school if he knows what the symbol is," said Mrs. O'Malley. "He studied archaeology at Oxford University in England."

"I think I will," said Lavender, then she helped clear the dirty dishes off the table and put them in the sink. Out the door she went, headed to school, holding the necklace in her hand so she could look at the charm as she walked.

Lavender reached school too late to talk to her teacher before class, so she had to wait the entire length of the day to ask Professor Priddle about her necklace. The minutes seemed like hours and the hours like days, until finally the bell rang.

Then Lavender had to wait for all the students to leave before she approached Professor Priddle at his desk with the charm necklace in her hand. He was reading and shuffling through papers, unaware of Lavender until she said, "Excuse me, Professor Priddle."

"Oh, my! You scared me, Lavender!" Professor Priddle startled, but his eyes quickly went toward the necklace. "Where did you get that magnificent old necklace? The symbolism is wonderful!"

"I'm not sure, Professor; I woke with it in my hand. I am wondering if you could tell me what this symbol is?"

"Woke with it in your hand? What an odd occurrence." The Professor took off his glasses, polished them, and then put them on the end of his nose. "Why, that appears to be some ancient symbol for water and sunlight. The circle with the horizontal line represents water, and the arrows represent sunlight and also knowledge. My guess is that this represents the way a rainbow is created as the arrows representing sunlight strike the water, refract from the curvature of the front of the drop and then reflect off the back of the drop, giving us all the beautiful colors."

"But where do all the colors come from?" asked Lavender.

"It is almost like magic, isn't it, Lavender?" he said with a smile. "Science tells us that when white light from the sun is split by a prism, or in this case a raindrop, then all the colors of the spectrum are released. This necklace probably symbolizes a rainbow. It looks very old, so take good care of it as it might be worth something."

A puzzled look overtook his face. "Hold on, where have I seen that symbol before?" He sat looking mystified for several seconds then his eyes went wide. "That's it!" He began to giggle, looking very gleeful and excited. He jumped up and shut the classroom door, then hurried back to his desk.

The Professor then looked Lavender straight in the eye. "I have something very important to show you,

Lavender, and you must keep it a secret. I am only sharing it with you because I believe the faeries gave you the necklace."

"The faeries? I don't understand." Lavender felt a flood of emotions. Excitement mixed with confusion and fear began spiraling in her gut.

The Professor simply ignored her question. "Now, Lavender, you must promise me that you will keep this a secret!"

Lavender hesitated only for a moment. "Absolutely, Professor Priddle, I promise never to tell anyone."

That was good enough for the Professor, who already knew Lavender to be perhaps his most honest and kind-hearted student. "Turn around and cover your eyes" he said. "I don't want anyone to know where I keep this."

Lavender turned away and covered her eyes. She heard the Professor walk a few steps, heard a small noise like a drawer opening, then heard him moving again, and a small click like a key in a lock. After a moment, she heard him come back to the desk.

"Lavender, you can open your eyes now."

Lavender opened her eyes and saw that the Professor was holding the oldest-looking book she had ever seen.

"I have never shown this to anyone in my life" the Professor said solemnly. "It's an ancient book probably written by faeries of Galtee Wood over ten thousand years ago. I can't tell you where I got this, but the information in this book is very, very secret."

The Professor turned the pages very carefully, as the book was brittle and the spine cracked. Lavender eagerly tried to catch glimpses of the strange writing and very old paintings. Suddenly his finger came down right in the middle of a page "Oh, my, my, my!" He glanced from the charm to the book, his head nodding with approval. Then he turned to Lavender again.

"For some reason, Lavender, the faeries think you deserve to be blessed. This is extremely rare, since they don't generally care for humans. You see, the book explains that faeries, leprechauns and all the other magical creatures born from the earth hold all the elements of the earth sacred. For the faeries of Galtee Wood, the most sacred elements of all are sunlight and water. Sunlight turns the darkness to light, allowing crops and plants to grow, flowers to blossom and life to form and flourish. Water is sacred because water also nourishes the crops and forests.

"Now when sunlight and water vapor collide, a rainbow forms, and the burst of brilliant colors is released like magic out of the sunlight. The occurrence of sunlight on a drop of rain creating a rainbow is so sacred and magical to the Galtee Wood faeries, probably nothing else surpasses it. The book says the faeries spent thousands of years trying to harness the power of the rainbow and its knowledge. The leprechauns learned how to open up the clouds and create rainbows to show their friends where they had left a pot of gold.

"However, it was an ancient faerie queen named Wisteria who tapped into the most powerful knowledge of the rainbow. She learned that each color represents a value such as love, curiosity, wisdom, strength, growth, passion and hope. Clearly, your necklace represents sunlight and water uniting, and the rainbow is represented by the arrow leaving the water. But what has me puzzled is the gold arrow leaving the raindrop. I have never seen that before."

Lavender was confused and nervously excited at the same time. "This all sounds amazing, Professor, but what does all this have to do with me? I don't understand."

The Professor impatiently waved his hand at Lavender. "Hold on, Lavender, I am trying to figure something out. Please let me think!"

The Professor turned several pages looking for an answer, then stopped and pointed at another page. There was a sketch of Lavender's necklace, this time with the golden arrow. Next to the sketch was a most inspiring image of a rainbow. But this rainbow was completely golden, glistening in a dark stormy sky. There were also faeries, elves, goblins and unicorns in the painting, which seemed to be looking at the golden rainbow and spiritually moved by seeing it. Lavender felt the painting had the look and feel of an old Renaissance masterpiece you might see in the Vatican in Rome.

Professor Priddle's eyes went wide, and his voice grew loud and very excited. "Lavender, this necklace represents the mysterious and extremely rare golden rainbow, which has never been seen by humans and probably vary rarely seen even in the faerie world. The importance of this necklace is paramount, its value beyond understanding! The golden rainbow will only appear when a human with a heart of gold walks through the most mystical places of the Galtee Woods or certain other faerie woods. The book speaks of the necklace and a ritual, but most of the words have faded and there are pages missing. I wish I could tell you more. What I wouldn't give to see a golden rainbow!"

Lavender's eyes grew big, and she moved closer to the book to get a better look. "This is all so exciting! I would like to see a golden rainbow as well. I hope Rose can see one, too. But why a golden rainbow? What of the other colors?"

The Professor turned to the beginning of the chapter on rainbows. "See here, Lavender, yellow is the part of sunlight that is the most powerful. It gives nutrition and energy to plants and helps them grow, but it also contains hidden wisdom. It represents the most pure love and kindness that lives inside the rays of the sun, and shines down upon the world directly from the great Creator.

"The book says that only when a heart of pure gold can be found will a rainbow turn pure golden, and only with the help of the good faerie Wisteria, who learned to unlock the wisdom of the rainbow over ten thousand years ago. She is the most powerful, wise faerie who ever lived in this part of the world. According to the book, she has been in search of a person with a heart of gold since she first unlocked the mystery of the rainbow."

He turned another page. "Oh, my! It says there has been only one other golden rainbow, and that was the one Wisteria first created. It says here that a few humans have come close, but no one has ever been pure and kind enough to be allowed to see a golden rainbow or to reach the end of one, where magic, beauty and great wisdom await."

"I wonder if this has to do with Rose?" Lavender wondered. "Maybe the faeries heard my wish last night to make her better. Maybe they are going to help her. What do you think, Professor Priddle?"

"Perhaps your wish did bring this on. Faeries love wishes, but rarely grant them. Often they will test a person to see what they are like deep inside before a wish is granted. If that is a real faerie necklace, then it's possible that you are at the start of a great journey, a magical one that you will never forget. The necklace was likely given to you by one of Wisteria's pixies while you slept. I think you have been chosen, Lavender!"

Lavender stared at the necklace. Could it really be a faerie gift? She looked up at Professor Priddle. "Is this all true, or is it make-believe?"

The Professor pulled off his glasses and laid his hands on Lavender's shoulders. "My brain and logical thinking tell me I am loopy, but my heart tells me this is all true. I can't say for sure, Lavender, but I spent half my life looking for this book when others said it didn't exist. Something tells me that necklace is real. Whatever it is, there is magic and wonder involved. Just keep in mind that once chosen by the Faeries of Galtee Wood, you're beginning a journey to a place of wonder, danger and enlightenment. Faeries don't play around; they will get to the bottom of your soul in ways you can't imagine!"

The Professor paused and a concerned look came over his face. He looked Lavender right in the eye. "Lavender, please beware of the dark faeries, as they will do anything to get their hands on that necklace." He reached into his desk drawer and pulled out a small leather pouch tied up at the top. "Take this; it's filled with iron dust. Iron repels faeries and can be used to break spells. Often what you see in the faerie realm may not be real, it may be the spell of a dark faerie. If you are smart enough to discover you are under a spell, take a pinch of iron dust into your hand and blow it into the face of the faerie you think is deceiving you."

Lavender took the pouch and put it carefully into her pocket.

"You'd better get home now," said the Professor. "And remember, your journey could start at any time. You will probably be approached by a good faerie who will instruct you as to what to do with the necklace. Follow the faerie's instructions carefully."

Lavender left school and began walking home in a light rain shower. As she rounded a small hill with several twisted oak trees growing on its side, she realized the sun had broken through the clouds, and a beautiful rainbow was forming over the green meadow and rolling hills just ahead.

"A rainbow! Just like my necklace!" thought Lavender. Remembering all the Professor had said, she wondered if the rainbow could be a sign. She ran like a racehorse toward the nearest end of the rainbow. Across the meadow and into the woods she went, jumped over an old rock wall, splashed through a stream, and came out on the far side of the woods, only to see that the rainbow looked just as far away as when she first saw it. Then a small cloud passed in front of the sun, and the rainbow disappeared.

Lavender stopped in her tracks and looked around. She was now standing at the entrance of the churchyard with its many old gravestones. There seemed to be roses lying near most of the gravestones, and the nearest grave

looked to be a child's, as sitting next to the headstone was a tattered stuffed bear. Lavender imagined what it would be like if Rose's name was there. The thought of Rose dying felt more real than ever before. She fell to the ground and began to weep for several minutes.

Then out of nowhere came a strange voice: "Hello, my dear girl!"

Lavender jumped, and looked around through her tears. A very odd little man, dressed all in green, was sitting on a gravestone right next to her.

Lavender jumped back and stared, then gathered herself. "Why, you're a Leprechaun aren't you?" She wiped her tears away and grappled with the reality that she really was talking to a Leprechaun.

The little man stood up and straightened his green jacket. "Allow me to introduce myself. I am Mr. McDarby. Our faerie Queen Wisteria received your wish to help Rose and thinks you could be worthy of her help. But first, you must prove you are worthy. You must give Rose the necklace by midnight tonight. If you do, Wisteria can help Rose. If you fail, the Banshee's cry will be heard outside her house tonight, and she will be gone forever."

Lavender began to perk up. "Really? I can save Rose? Oh, thank you, thank you!" Lavender reached toward the Leprechaun to hug him, but he quickly jumped out of reach. Lavender remembered that Leprechauns take great care never to let a human catch them. "I'd better go right away!"

"Not so fast!" said Mr. McDarby. "The dark faeries know you will be taking the necklace to Rose's house. They are strongest after sunset, and they could be behind any tree or rock ready to deceive you and take the necklace. You must promise to give the necklace to no one but Rose."

"I promise! I will give the necklace to Rose and absolutely no one else! But it's only three o'clock, why do I need to worry about dark faeries?" asked Lavender.

"Dark faeries can be out in the daytime, too," said Mr. McDarby. "If you see any good faeries along the way, follow them. They may know that a dark faerie is near, and they will lead you to a safer way to Rose's house. And remember, you have until midnight, or Rose will surely die. The Banshee has let it be known that Rose is scheduled to die at midnight tonight."

Before Lavender could ask any more questions, he disappeared into the grass and was gone.

Chapter 3

Lavender stood for a moment, trying to grasp what had just happened.

"I just met a Leprechaun! Why, it was just as Professor Priddle said. A good faerie came and gave me my instructions. Wait until I tell him that Wisteria is real! And that she is still around! But first, I need to go right away and save Rose."

From there in the churchyard, she could go to Rose's house by a road that wound across the meadows and through the village. Or she could take a shortcut she knew through a corner of Galtee Wood, and get to Rose even sooner. She looked at the sun, climbing down through the clouds in the western sky. She still had plenty of time before sunset, when the dark faeries would come out. She turned and started running along the shortcut path, and soon she reached the edge of Galtee Wood.

Following the path into the trees, Lavender looked around and saw that the woods looked different today. They were eerily silent and dark, with tangled branches, and very little light reaching the forest floor from the dense treetops above. She slowed to a walk for several minutes.

A harsh "Caw! Caw! Caw!" broke the silence. A black raven perched in the twisted branches above her head. Lavender had heard stories that seeing a raven meant that death could be coming. She glanced nervously around the woods. The raven flew off abruptly, calling out again, "Caw, caw, caw!" Its voice echoed through the otherwise silent woods.

"Maybe it was a bad idea to come this way," Lavender thought.

Concerned about the safety of the charm necklace, Lavender remembered the Professor's pouch of iron dust. She took off the necklace and hid it in the pouch to protect it from bad faeries. "I hope no dark faeries are watching me and playing tricks on me."

She began to run again, looking from side to side, even behind her to make sure no one or nothing un-human was after her. Then, just ahead in the darkness of the trees, a loud crashing startled her. Something large was rushing through the trees. She saw a flash of white, then a white horse partly hidden behind the twisted tree trunks ahead. Lavender's mouth dropped wide open when she saw a beautiful, twisted horn growing out of its head.

"Why, it's a Unicorn!" She felt her heart skip a beat.

It appeared strong and handsome, with piercing yellow eyes. Just its presence helped Lavender feel safe and comforted. It stood for several seconds looking right at her, and then it bounded back into the woods.

Lavender knew from her stories that Unicorns were always pure and good. "There must be danger around and he wants me to follow him, just as the Leprechaun Mr. McDarby said," she thought. Then she noticed several stones along the path with ancient markings on them. "I sure don't like the look of those stones and the markings on them. For all I know they are a warning sign from the faeries."

Lavender reached the tree where the Unicorn had been standing. He was gone, and all she could see was dark forest climbing the steep slope above the path. Just beyond the tree, she found some white hair caught on a branch. Lavender gently pulled it off the branch, hardly believing that she was holding the hair of a unicorn. In that instant, she saw the white flash of the unicorn far up the slope.

Lavender followed. With each step she kept an eye on the forest around her, worried that a bad faerie could jump out at any time and take the necklace. At the top of the ridge, she found another clump of white hair and saw the unicorn's hoof prints leading down into a narrow, heavily wooded valley that she had never seen before. She could hear rushing water far below.

"I guess I should follow him," she thought, "but he is leading me away from Rose's house. I hope in leading me away from dark faeries, he doesn't take me too far off."

As Lavender pushed on down the hill, storm clouds began to swirl and churn above her. Wind whistled though the woods, and dead branches above creaked and swayed. The forest grew as dark as late evening, though it was still mid afternoon. At last she reached a fast-moving stream at the bottom of the ravine. She looked up and down the banks of the stream, but found no trace of hoof prints or any sign of where the Unicorn had gone.

Lavender sat down to rest on a small rock. She was irritated at the disappearance of the Unicorn, and more than a little concerned that the creature had taken her so far from Rose's house. Looking around, she realized that she didn't even know which way she had come. Both ridges above looked the same, and she was sure the stream had been running in the opposite direction when she first reached it. It was as if the valley had spun around her. Lavender wondered if the faeries of the forest were trying to trick her.

"I think I came down this side of the valley," she thought, but she was far from sure. Another gust of wind rushed along the ridge high above, catching dead leaves and blowing them through the twisted trees. Lavender was beginning to be afraid she was lost, and that bad faeries were going to take the necklace away before she could give it to Rose.

"I can't just sit here, I have to find a way out," she thought. "I came uphill to get here, so I guess I will just have to head downstream and hope I hit the road near where I went into the woods. The stream must eventually leave the mountains and reach someplace near the village."

She got up and started hiking along the stream, hoping she was headed in the right direction. The wind blew harder and colder. Lavender hunkered down to stay warm, as dark, swirling clouds began to drop rain over the forest. All around her, lighting began to flash, lighting up the woods every few seconds.

Lavender opened her umbrella to break the wind and pelting rain. Even though it was raining hard now, she felt she needed to move quickly to find her way out of the woods. She tried to run along the side of the stream, but her feet slipped and stumbled over the rocks and wet leaves, and branches clawed at her clothes.

Then with a huge bang, lightning struck a tree almost over her head, and it crashed down into the ravine only a few yards in front of her. Lavender screamed! Her whole body shook from head to toe.

"That tree almost fell on me! I have to find some shelter from this storm," she thought.

She looked around, desperate to get away from the lightning and the rain. Beyond the fallen tree, the stream went through a narrow gorge between two rocky ledges. She scrambled along the bank until she came to the rocks, and there, as she hoped, was an overhanging rock making a little shelter.

Lavender crawled under the overhang, and curled up in a hollow among the rocks, hugging her coat around

her, and holding the pouch with the necklace charm safe in one hand. She was wet, cold and shivering, and now she noticed she was really hungry, too. It must be hours since she left the Professor after school, and she hadn't eaten anything since lunch.

Lightning flashed again and again, lighting up the little gorge outside her shelter. Across from her, a waterfall poured down over high rocks and into the stream, and formed a large pool. At the lower end, the rock cliffs ended, and the stream ran away into the trees again. With another lightning flash, Lavender saw moss-covered stones along the sides of the pool, and water lilies blooming among the lily pads.

"Rose would love this little pool," she thought. "I wish I could show it to her. I wish I was with her right now, giving her the necklace." Tears welled up at the thought of Rose, and Lavender put her head in her arms and began to sob. She was so grief-stricken and exhausted that before she knew it, she cried herself to sleep.

There she lay under the overhang beside the lily pond, while the lightning and thunder moved away, the winds grew calm, and the rain turned to a drizzle, then stopped. The woods were so quiet; the only sound was the rushing of the waterfall.

Then something moved in the trees beside the pool. Dozens of light sparkles began to move out of the woods and surround Lavender. They were tiny faeries. Several other harmless forest faeries came cautiously out of the forest and from behind rocks to see Lavender. Even water pixies like tiny mermaids poked their heads out of the pool to look at her, and some slid up on the mossy rocks and the lily pads to get a better view.

A small pixie landed next to Lavender. It giggled as it touched Lavender's hair to feel its soft texture. Others climbed to her knees to see her face and clothes. Rarely did they get the chance to see a human this closely. Though the forest was dark, light from many of the faeries gave the scene an enchanting look. A group of faeries circled around Lavender and began to dance, singing and laughing.

Then from upstream came a mighty crash. The faeries scattered instantly.

Lavender woke and opened her eyes to the sight of the Unicorn standing on the opposite side of the lily pond. It was looking right at her as if to tell her to come.

Relief flooded her. The Unicorn hadn't deserted her after all. She scrambled down out of her shelter.

"What now?" she said to the Unicorn. "Where is Rose's house? I am running out of time to save Rose!"

The beautiful white creature waded into the pool, and then it walked right under the waterfall and disappeared from sight.

"There must be a cave behind those falls and maybe a shortcut or a magic doorway to Rose's house," Lavender thought. Anything seemed possible with a Unicorn.

She waded into the pool and splashed her way to the foot of the waterfall, then held her breath, and plunged in. For one step, the power from the falls was heavy on her head and shoulders as the water crashed down upon her, and she could hear nothing but the roar of the falling water. Then she cleared the falls, let out her breath and wiped water out of her eyes. Directly ahead was a long, dark, empty cave with a small stream running out of it.

"Where did the Unicorn go?" thought Lavender. She began walking into the darkness. The soft light coming in through the waterfall grew dimmer and dimmer, until Lavender could hardly see her hand in front of her face. Water dripped onto her head from the cave ceiling.

"What a horrible, cold, creepy place for a Unicorn to live," she thought, and then she bumped into a rock wall in the darkness. She felt along the wall for a few steps.

The cave seemed to be turning in a different direction. "I don't feel good about this place or the Unicorn; I am going to go back."

Just then, a most wicked laugh echoed from the dark passage ahead. Lavender felt the hairs on her neck stick straight up. She began to run back toward the waterfall. As she ran, she heard something splashing behind her, getting closer and closer. Lavender tripped, and then violently fell into the shallow stream. Before she could get up, something grabbed onto her ankle with very big strong hands! Lavender looked back and saw a brown face with horns and yellow eyes—just like the Unicorn's eyes.

"Got you!" cried the creature, and it dragged Lavender back into the cave. Lavender was so frightened that at first she couldn't even find enough breath to scream. Then she found her breath and her wits. She began to let out one bloodcurdling scream after another, and kicked and struggled to stop the creature from dragging her.

"Let me go!" cried Lavender. "Who are you?"

"Quiet, you dreadful child! I am the Pooka of these parts of the woods. I am going to cook you up to go with my trout stew tonight, and use the magical powers of that necklace."

Lavender fell silent with shock. She knew the Pooka was more feared than any other kind of faerie. It could take any shape, and it usually appeared as a sleek, dark horse with piercing yellow eyes and a long, wild mane. But this time, the Pooka had appeared as a Unicorn, and led her into this trap.

"All this time I followed you, because I thought you were helping me to get to Rose," said Lavender.

Though she struggled with all her strength, the Pooka dragged her to a round, open cave. Torches burned there, and a giant cauldron filled with boiling water sat on a fire. Beside the fire stood a rough wooden table and chair, and beyond was a door in the far wall of the cave. At the bottom of the room was a little pond filled with trout. Twisted tree roots grew along the walls of the cave, and water dripped all around.

The Pooka dropped Lavender to the ground next to the cauldron, and for the first time Lavender could see its face. It was very ugly and brown in color, and its clothes were old and tattered. It wore a simple tunic that was tied in the middle with rope and smelled like fish. Its eyes were the most striking, glowing yellow in the dimly lit room, especially when they caught the firelight.

The Pooka began slicing roots and salamanders and throwing them into the boiling pot. Then it lurched over to the pond, grabbed several trout with its big, stubby fingers, and threw them into the pot, too.

"Are you are going to eat them like that?" asked Lavender "I have never seen anyone eat fish without taking the guts out."

"Of course! I will eat you the same way!" the Pooka said. "But first I will take your necklace!"

The Pooka began pulling and poking at Lavender's clothes to find where she had hidden the necklace.

"Get away from me!" Lavender yelled, struggling against the Pooka's grip.

"Got it!" The Pooka grabbed the hidden pouch that held the necklace. The next instant, a big spark shot out. The Pooka gave a screech of pain and yanked its hand away.

Lavender's plan of using the pouch to protect the necklace had worked, but she knew she was still in a horrible bind, and Rose's time was running out quickly.

"Well, Lavender, it looks like we are both in a bad spot," said the Pooka. "You need to get to Rose's house by midnight, or she will die. I want that necklace, but it seems to be protected. I will make you an offer where we both win. If you give me the necklace, I will grant you and Rose friendship and happiness for a thousand years."

"You are lying! Rose will die without the necklace. Mr. McDarby the Leprechaun told me so," said Lavender.

The Pooka's eyebrows went up. "No, she won't," it said confidently. "Look into my pool and see what I will give you in exchange for the necklace."

The Pooka led her over to the fish pond. It waved its hand over the water, and Lavender saw herself and Rose together placing flowers on Mrs. Dougall's doorstep, then running and hiding as the old widow came out to find the flowers. No other memory meant this much to Lavender, especially since she knew it meant so much to Rose. Lavender stared into the pool. Rose was smiling and laughing, looking her old self again, full of energy and kindness, with a bounce in her step. The wonderful feelings of being with Rose, feelings of contentment and happiness, bubbled up inside Lavender, a thousand times more powerful than they had been in real life.

"I will grant to you and Rose, happiness for a thousand years!" said the Pooka.

Lavender knew that a faerie in a tight spot would grant a wish to get what it needed. Even an evil faerie like the Pooka would have to keep its promise. But when she looked into the pool, her feelings of happiness were overwhelming. If she gave the Pooka the necklace, what she saw in the pool would become real, and Rose would be saved.

She reached into the pouch that held the necklace, still staring at the vision in the pool. Then her fingers touched the charm, and she remembered Mr. McDarby saying, "You must promise to give the necklace to no one but Rose." And herself answering, "I promise!"

She had given her word to Mr. McDarby. She thought of the Professor and the book, and the great history of the necklace and Wisteria and the golden rainbow. It was clearly not meant for human hands unless Wisteria allowed it to be. She knew she needed to try to save Rose the right way, even with the odds against her.

She pulled the pouch away. "No! Even if I could be friends with Rose for a million years and feel this happy, I would be going against my word. It's not my necklace, and you can't have it!"

Veins popped out in the Pooka's forehead and it hissed, exposing sharp teeth. It violently grabbed again for the pouch, but was zapped again by the iron dust. It screamed in pain, lost its footing, and fell back away from Lavender.

Lavender saw instantly that now was her only chance. She would be caught if she ran back through the dark twisting cave, so she had to try the door beyond the cauldron. Dodging around the crouching goblin, she grabbed the door handle. The door opened, she rushed through and slammed it shut behind her.

Chapter 4

With her back to the door, Lavender turned to look for a place to hide in the forest. But the forest was gone.

She found herself standing beside a large, slow-moving river in a meadow that looked nothing like the narrow valley of the waterfall. Worried the Pooka would soon follow, Lavender reached for the pouch and quickly turned around toward the door. It was gone, and so was the steep hillside. In its place were moss-covered rocks and trees on a gentle slope.

"Strange!" thought Lavender. "Maybe that was a test and it's over now. I beat the Pooka."

The weather, too, had changed completely. The storm was gone, and the sun was shining. All around her were large weeping willows and wide grassy slopes. The river was covered with lily pads and blossoms, and elegant swans floated beneath the willows in the soft sunlight.

Lavender felt relieved to be safe from the Pooka, but she was still lost, and the sun was so low that she knew she must have lost a lot of time. "I have to find Rose! It will be dark soon, too."

Lavender determined that her best chance to find a town was to follow the river. She began walking briskly because she was too tired to run, especially as she was very hungry. Even though the river was pleasant to look at, she was well aware that the coming of nighttime would bring more bad faeries out and about. She found herself constantly looking at the sinking sun and becoming more and more worried. She emptied a small amount of iron dust from the pouch into her hand, just to be prepared for more Pookas or, so close to a river, perhaps a Shellycoat or Kelpie or some other evil water faerie could be around.

After she had been walking a long while, Lavender saw something small and bright dancing toward her along the river's surface. As it grew closer, she saw that it was a girl no bigger than a dragonfly, like a tiny water nymph. It twirled and gracefully skipped across the water, sometimes landing on lily pads, then jumping high into the air and coming down softly on the top of another lily pad or a small rock or even a turtle's shell. Below it in the clear dark waters, large trout darted back and forth, excited by the light coming from the tiny nymph.

It drew even with Lavender and paused for an instant to look at her, then it danced away upstream, waving for Lavender to follow.

"Look at you! So elegant and graceful, such a wonderful dancer!" Lavender cried. "You must be a good faerie trying to show me how to get to Rose's house!" She turned back and began chasing after the nymph. The nymph twirled and leaped and skipped, and Lavender scrambled along the river bank after it, giggling with excitement at its grace and charm.

All at once, the little nymph stopped moving upstream, and danced across the water toward Lavender. It waved its hand, pointing across the river. There, rising above the trees and reflecting in the mirror-like waters of the river, was a majestic castle. The nymph waved its hand again, and instantly Lavender was no longer wearing her school clothes, but a beautiful gown fit for a princess.

Lavender looked over herself, noticing the intricate designs and splendor of the dress. "Why, it's beautiful! Thank you so much!"

The nymph flew to a nearby bush with purple blossoms, picked a flower and handed it to Lavender.

"Wisteria!" it whispered in Lavender's ear. Leaping to the water, it began to dance again, heading toward the castle and waving to Lavender to follow.

"This must be where Wisteria lives!" thought Lavender. Just as she was wondering how she could cross the river to reach the castle, she noticed something approaching her from the river through the golden mist. It was an empty swan boat that seemed to be coming straight to her.

The elegant swan boat stopped at the shore next to her, and the little dancing water nymph signaled for Lavender to step aboard. As soon as she was standing in the boat, it took off gently by itself and glided toward the castle. Soon Lavender found herself gliding under the trees around the castle, and through a passageway that ended in a flight of steps leading into the castle. There, a handsome elf guard in uniform waited for the boat to dock. He bowed and extended his hand to help her to the steps.

"Come with me, Lavender, Wisteria is waiting for you in the ballroom," said the guard. They walked up the steps then along an elegant hallway bustling with many different faeries. Lavender was overwhelmed with the beauty of the castle and all the charming faeries around her. It was like a dream.

Eventually they reached a huge ballroom with golden walls. All along one side of the room was a table covered with beautiful desserts and prepared meats, fruit and salads. The room was full of faeries in bright clothes, dancing away. But the moment Lavender reached the door, everyone stopped dancing and looked toward her, smiling and bowing. The crowd of faeries opened a path down the middle of the ballroom. Across the way, Lavender could see a raised platform where stood a faerie Queen dressed in a most beautiful purple gown.

Beside the Queen was a sight Lavender could hardly fathom.

"Oh, my gosh! It's Rose!" yelled Lavender. There stood Rose, smiling and waving at her. She ran across the ballroom, and she and Rose embraced for several seconds. "Rose, you're all better!"

"Yes, your wish and Wisteria saved my life," said Rose. "Allow me to introduce you to the Queen." Rose turned Lavender toward Wisteria. "Queen Wisteria, this is Lavender, my very best friend!"

Lavender looked at Wisteria's beautiful face. "Thank you, thank you, Queen Wisteria! How can I ever repay you for this? You gave me back my best friend!"

Wisteria smiled down at Lavender, stroking her hair. "You can repay me by having a feast, dancing and enjoying your time with Rose. Then we will finish off the evening by watching the first glorious golden rainbow to shine above Galtee Wood in ten thousand years, and, of course, the treasure at its end, which you and Rose can share."

Lavender and Rose looked at each other and smiled. Wisteria then asked Lavender and Rose to come forward for the sacred ritual of the passing of the necklace to Rose. Trumpets began to play, and everyone erupted in cheers, applauding Lavender for her bravery and pure heart in bringing the necklace to her friend and getting past the trickery of the Pooka.

The two girls stood upon the platform in front of Wisteria, as she began to read from an old scroll telling of the ancient and sacred ritual of the golden rainbow and the recipient of its great treasures. Wisteria ended her reading, and then instructed

Lavender to give the necklace to Rose.

Lavender reached into her pouch to get the necklace, but as she touched it, she began to feel strange about giving it up. Her thoughts went to Professor Priddle and his warning about the bad faeries, and how they would do anything to get the necklace. She looked carefully at her friend. Rose looked perfectly normal and as beautiful as ever.

"Handing this necklace over to anyone is the biggest decision I have ever had to face in my life," Lavender thought. "I'd better be completely sure this is Rose, because if it's a faerie trick, Rose will die."

Quickly Lavender pulled out her hand and handed the whole pouch to Rose. The instant Rose's fingertips touched it, a spark burst out, and Rose snatched her hand away. Lavender took the pouch back, reached in for a handful of iron dust, and threw it into the faces of Rose and the Queen. The crowd looked shocked, as did Rose and Wisteria!

"What are you doing, Lavender?" screamed Rose.

Lavender looked at them both, still in their same form, and felt embarrassed and horrified at what she had done. "I am sorry, Rose, I heard the spark, and your hand went back. I thought it was a trick. Please forgive me, Wisteria!" she pleaded.

Then she saw that Rose and Wisteria were beginning to change. Their features were wasting away, and they were rapidly changing form! Before Lavender's eyes, the gilded walls of the ballroom vanished, and everyone around her turned from elegantly dressed faeries to twisted, skinny gnomes. The beautiful banquet turned to rotted foods that were dried up, moldy and covered in dust. Wisteria and Rose were gone, and in their place stood the two largest gnomes.

The iron dust had broken their spell over Lavender. There had never been a real castle or beautiful faeries, only the illusion. Now all that remained were a few ruined castle walls and the gnomes who had tried to trick Lavender into giving them the necklace.

Holding the iron dust in her hand, Lavender threatened all the gnomes with it. They quickly backed off. Lavender ran out of the castle ruin toward the river. It was no longer beautiful and surrounded with weeping willows, but was a foggy, creepy swamp full of dead trees.

Lavender ran.

Chapter 5

She ran and ran until she had to stop to catch her breath.

"I must have lost at least another hour," she thought. "I have no idea how to get to Rose's house, and the evil faeries seem to be everywhere trying to trick me into giving them the necklace. This is beginning to seem impossible." Lavender took a deep breath, gathered her thoughts and reached down deep inside herself for strength. "I have to be strong for Rose. There is still time. I must save Rose if it's the last thing I ever do!"

She looked around. Now there was no sign of the dark forest or the swampy river. In every direction she saw rolling, grassy hills under a clear sky with just a few puffy clouds. Small groves of trees stood here and there. Then she noticed a footpath that seemed to wind away through the hills.

"Oh, thank goodness! This path must lead somewhere," she thought, and immediately began to walk along it.

The path turned to follow a small stream running through the open meadows. As she walked beside the stream, Lavender could see frogs, salamanders and trout hiding under the undercut banks or gliding into the sunlit water. The scenery was the prettiest Lavender had seen in her whole life; there was a magical beauty to everything around her.

After a while the path rounded a steep hill, and Lavender saw ahead of her a tree so big that someone had built a home in its trunk. A small porch led to a brightly painted door with cute round windows next it. Flowers grew in planters under the windows and along the walkway to the porch. The tree house looked so pleasant that Lavender walked up the steps and knocked on the door.

"I hope these people can tell me how to get to Rose's house," she thought. "Funny how the door is so small." She was several feet taller than the door when standing next to it.

A few seconds passed, then the door opened, and to Lavender's surprise, there stood the leprechaun Mr. McDarby.

"Why, Lavender, what on earth are you doing here? Did you give the necklace to Rose?" he asked.

Filled to the brim with relief, Lavender grabbed hold of Mr. McDarby and gave him a huge hug as tears began to pool in her eyes. "I am so glad to see you, Mr. McDarby! I am completely lost, and the wicked faeries are all over the place trying to trick me, and Rose only has a few hours left! Can you tell me how to get to her house?"

"You poor child! Don't worry; you are actually quite close to Rose's house. It's just an hour's walk from here. I can point you in the right direction, but first let's get you warmed up and get some food in you."

"Are you sure I have enough time?" asked Lavender.

"You look famished and cold and you have been wet. You will need to eat to have the strength to make it to Rose's. You have plenty of time," he said.

Mr. McDarby led Lavender up the narrow stairs into his eating nook, which was the coziest place Lavender had ever seen, with rustic furniture that seemed to be carved right out of the inside of the tree. Many house plants stood on the windowsills, and beautiful sunlight coming in through the windows cast a warm glow on the room. Lavender was amazed that she was able to fit, and that she was actually inside a tree.

"Now you sit right down and rest while I get you something to eat," said Mr. McDarby, and went through a doorway into another room.

Lavender sat down with a huge sense of relief, knowing that her chances to save Rose were looking much brighter. For a while, she looked around at the paintings on the walls. Then she noticed how the sunlight had moved in the room and she began to worry. Mr. McDarby seemed to be taking a very long time to prepare the food.

Finally he shuffled in with a tray of delicious looking fruits and meats and a mug full of strawberry nectar.

"Eat up, Lavender!" He put the tray down on a table in front of her. "Oh, but leave room for dessert, as I have the most wonderful chocolate cake you will ever taste! Maybe once Rose is better you can bring her by to try some, too!"

"I would love to bring Rose here to meet you!" said Lavender, as she quickly ate up everything in front of her. When she was finished, she started to get up. Mr. McDarby stopped her.

"You mustn't go until you eat some cake," he said. He scooted out and returned with a huge slice of layered chocolate cake on a plate. It did look wonderful, but Lavender hesitated.

"Oh, thank you, Mr. McDarby, but I really must be going," she said. "It's going to be dark before I get to Rose's house and I don't want to deal with any more bad faeries." She looked toward the door then looked back at Mr. McDarby, who stood there sadly holding the cake. Lavender felt she had hurt his feelings. "Well, okay, Mr. McDarby, I will have a piece, as it looks amazing! How about if I just eat it on the way?" she asked.

"At least take a nibble so I can see if you like it," Mr. McDarby pleaded.

Lavender took a small bite. "Wow! That is wonderful! That is so rich, and the frosting is so creamy! You can count on Rose and me coming back! Now I really must be going."

A big smile came across Mr. McDarby's face. "Take the rest with you. You can eat it on the way." He put the piece of cake in her hand, and then he opened the door for Lavender and pointed the way. "You see those two hills over there? Those are sacred to the good woodland faeries, and the bad faeries generally avoid them. When you reach the hills, you will see the village and the road

to Rose's house. If you go now, you can take the path through the old forest, because it's much shorter than taking the long road around. Lots of bad faeries live in the old forest, but they are all night dwellers and can't stand the sight of the sun. As long as you reach the hills before the sun goes down, you will be safe."

Lavender hugged Mr. McDarby, careful not to get cake on him. "Thank you! I should have no problem making it to Rose's house now."

"You're welcome my dear! But remember, if you don't reach the old growth forest before sunset, don't go in there. It's much too dangerous to enter at night, and you will most certainly never make it out to see your family again!"

Lavender felt blackness shudder through her veins. "But if I go around, how much longer will it take? Will I still get to Rose on time?"

Mr. McDarby looked up at Lavender with big eyes. "Going around the forest will take many, more hours. If you go that way, you might not reach Rose's house before the Banshee, but at least you will make it home alive. It's not worth risking your life to save Rose by going into those woods at night!" He put his hand on her arm. "But don't worry, Lavender. It's only an hour's walk through the forest to the sacred hills, and you have almost an hour of daylight left, so you should be fine. Good luck!"

Lavender thanked Mr. McDarby again and set out on the path toward the forest and the two hills, taking another bite of the chocolate cake. The sun was already casting long shadows across the path, which could be seen disappearing into the dark shadows of the old growth forest ahead.

As Lavender walked toward the gnarled old trees, something peculiar happened. The trees seemed to stay the same distance away, no matter how long she walked. It was like chasing a rainbow. Lavender began to run, and for few minutes the forest seemed to be drawing closer, but when she stopped to rest, it looked as far off as ever.

"Oh no! The faeries are playing tricks on me again," she thought. "The sun will be gone soon, and I haven't even reached the forest. How will I make it through before dark?"

Then suddenly the forest was right in front of her. The path forked, and one fork went into the shadow of the trees, while the other wound along the edge of the forest. A signpost stood beside the path with two signs on it. The one pointing into the forest said, "Village,

30 minutes." The sign pointing around the forest said, "Village, 3 hours."

Lavender turned and saw that the sun was already sinking behind the rolling fields.

"Oh, dear!" she thought. "It's already getting dark. I took too long to get here."

She looked into the blackness of the forest. The old trees hung like huge, gnarled ghouls over the path. Some looked half dead, and many sent large, twisted roots across the path.

"I don't like the looks of this forest, and I don't want to get caught in there by the wicked faeries. Mr. McDarby warned me that if I go in after dark, I will never make it out! But if I go around, I won't reach Rose before the Banshee."

Lavender put her hand inside the pouch and felt the charm and the iron dust. Maybe that would keep her safe. She hesitated for several more seconds, and then took a very deep breath. "This is it, Rose. All that stands between you and getting better is the next mile, and whatever danger lurks in these woods after dark. I have to go in. It's the only way to save you."

Then she marched into the darkness of the forest.

Chapter 6

The forest was very silent,
with only the sound of her own feet.

She didn't even hear any birds.

"This place is so creepy! It's much worse than the woods where I met the Pooka," she thought, and picked up her pace.

A strange sensation began fluttering through her veins. Her legs felt tired, then, all of a sudden, a sharp pain shot through her gut. She slumped down, clutching her middle with a cry. She was still holding a piece of Mr. McDarby's cake, but her desire for it was gone. She threw it to the ground and continued on her way. But she felt herself growing weaker with each step, and constant intense pain still twisted in her gut. With each step the pain grew, and her energy dissipated at an alarming rate.

"I have to rest, or I will never make it to Rose's house." Lavender sat down on a rock next to a small spring, and used her hands to drink.

As she sat there, she began to feel that she was being watched or followed. Then she heard something crackling through the woods nearby. Fear gripped her whole body. She used all her strength to get up and slowly continued her way through the woods. The pain in her stomach had now spread all through her, and her breath was growing wheezy and shallow. Every step was torture. Only her fear of the woods and her desire to save Rose kept her moving.

The forest was now almost completely dark. The moon shone through the twisted branches above, casting a subtle light on the pathway ahead. Lavender stopped and took several painful breaths before she began to walk again. Then she heard a moaning cry in the distance. While faint, it was piercing, like a wounded cat lying in the forest. Lavender felt the hair on the back of her neck stand up. She knew instantly it was the cry of the Banshee on her way to Rose's house.

"Oh, this is terrible!" thought Lavender. "I have to move faster! I can't let her get to Rose before me."

Lavender struggled forward, feeling that she had exhausted every muscle in her body and every last ounce of energy. She tripped over a root and fell hard on the ground. As she lay, trying desperately to get up in her feeble state, she saw something moving through the woods.

A pale female figure emerged from the trees and came toward her, seeming almost to float over the rocky forest floor. A white cloak like a cobweb clung to the woman's tall, thin body. Her face was pale, her eyes red, and she slowly drew a brush through silver-grey hair that streamed to the ground. In an instant, Lavender knew this was the Banshee. Rose's chances to live were vanishing.

The Banshee floated within a few feet of Lavender and opened her pale, cracked lips, showing teeth twisted and sharp. She gave a long, piercing cry that echoed through the woods. Lavender was horrified, and the piercing cry caused the pain inside her to shoot through every inch of her body.

Lavender grabbed a twisted tree branch, dragged herself up off the ground and desperately tried to run along the path. She had to reach Rose's house before the Banshee.

After only a few steps, she fell among the tree roots, with pain that was beyond description.

"I must get up, I must save Rose!" Lavender said to herself, ignoring the tears of grief and horror running down her cheeks.

She looked up and saw that the Banshee had stopped right beside her and was looking down at her. Lavender tried to crawl away, feeling as if she herself were dying. But she had no more energy to move.

"Is this how Rose has been feeling?" she wondered.

The Banshee gave another terrible cry that echoed through the forest and made Lavender cower.

She had to reach deep for the strength to speak. "Why have you stopped?" she gasped. "Are you here for Rose? Or for me?"

The Banshee let out one more blood-curdling scream. Then it spoke in a voice like a dying old woman. "I am crying for you, Lavender Blue O'Malley. Your friend Rose is almost completely well now. You have taken her illness by eating Mr. McDarby's cake. Wasn't that what you wished for? That you could take Rose's place?"

Lavender leaned her head back against the tree roots, her mind and body exhausted and in horrible pain. She remembered that she had asked to take Rose's place. She nodded in agreement, too weak now to speak.

The Banshee wailed again. Tears ran from her bloodshot eyes down her corpse-white cheeks. At last the terrible cry ended. The Banshee stretched out a hand that held a small vial full of liquid.

"This potion can cure you if you wish," she said. "If you drink it, the illness and pain you are feeling will instantly be taken from your body and sent back to Rose's body. She will die, and you will live. You are under no obligation to save Rose; today is the day I am supposed to escort her to the next world. What do you choose, Lavender Blue?"

Lavender turned her face toward the moonlight. She thought about Rose and Rose's parents and all they had been through. She remembered the tears of Rose's mother, knowing her daughter was dying. Then she thought about her own parents and Rose, and how they would feel once she was gone.

The pain in her body was now unbearable. She could hardly grasp that Rose had suffered this way for so long. She thought, "I can't let Rose go through this again."

"What is your choice?" said the Banshee.

Lavender struggled to lift her eyes and whisper, "I choose to die. I chose to take Rose's place."

The Banshee let out a screaming cry so loud it was heard throughout the forest. "It is done," she said. "Rose lives, and you die. Farewell, Lavender." Then she drew back and slowly glided away into the trees.

As Lavender looked where the Banshee had gone, she noticed faint lights moving through the trees toward her. When they came near, she saw that they were dozens of woodland faeries, their eyes all filled with tears at seeing Lavender dying.

"Don't cry, sweet ones," Lavender whispered. "Rose is all better now. My dear friend lives." Lavender gasped for a breath and finally her eyes closed. There Lavender lay in the moonlight with all the faeries around her still weeping and wiping tears away.

Slowly the good faeries gathered around Lavender and lifted her up. They carried her body out of the dark forest and to the top of the tallest sacred hill, which was crowned with a ring of ancient standing stones. There they laid her in the ring on an ancient stone table, then gathered woodland flowers to place around

her body. Soon more faeries arrived, holding candles, and floated around her. As the stars circled in the sky, they mourned her under the full moon.

Just before midnight, as the moon climbed directly overhead, a small, bright light arose from a nearby vale and came toward the sacred hilltop. Closer and closer it came, until the woodland faeries saw a stunningly beautiful pixie hovering above Lavender. With a wave of its hand, the pixie sprinkled wisteria and lavender petals across Lavender's body, petals that shimmered as if they were filled with faerie magic. The light flickered across her body, bringing color to her pale cheeks.

Then the pixie whispered to a Brownie standing nearby. He listened carefully, and slowly a big smile formed across his face. He jumped up onto a rock and spoke in a loud voice to all the faeries.

"I have great news! Lavender is not dead; Wisteria sent this faerie to save her! She has passed all the tests, and tomorrow a golden rainbow will shine above Galtee Wood for the first time in over ten thousand years! Spread the word so everyone will be there to greet Lavender as she rides to the end of the golden rainbow. Let us all celebrate, for a heart of gold has been found!"

All the faeries began to clap and cheer. One by one they came and kissed Lavender on the cheek as she slept, then flew away to their homes in trees and holes. They had to prepare for a great day of celebration!

Chapter 7

All night Lavender slept atop the hill, surrounded by all the gifts the faeries had brought her.

Morning broke, and just as warm rays of sunlight touched Lavender's face, a majestic Unicorn climbed to the top of the sacred hill through fields of wildflowers. He nudged Lavender with his muzzle until she began to wake. As her eyes focused, they fell on the Unicorn, and she sat straight up, staring suspiciously. Out of habit, she reached for the pouch and the necklace to protect herself.

"Be at ease, Lavender," said the Unicorn. "You have passed all of Wisteria's tests, and Rose is now healed. You took her illness into your body, and Wisteria's magic washed it from your body."

The Unicorn's eyes were as blue as a sapphire crystal, with not a tinge of Pooka yellow. He lowered his head and let her pet his face and touch his horn. As she touched it, a magical, peaceful feeling took over her body, and she knew that this was no Pooka, but a noble and pure Unicorn. Then she knew for sure her journey was near its end. Tears welled up in her eyes as she realized Rose was all better, and all the darkness was turning to sunshine.

The Unicorn turned sideways next to the stone table, inviting Lavender to get on his back. As soon as she was on, the Unicorn took off! Down the hill he galloped, through an open meadow and a shifting sea of wildflowers, then up another hillside. Lavender was amazed that the Unicorn's stride was so smooth; she hardly felt like they were moving, and she didn't have to hold on at all.

Storm clouds were mushrooming into the sky overhead, and the wind was kicking up. Lightning flashed, and then a loud clap of thunder echoed across the mountains and valleys. Soon they were riding through the rain, but Lavender didn't get wet. The rain beaded up in silver drops and rolled right off her clothes and skin.

They came to a rocky hilltop and the Unicorn halted. Down below was a misty vale checker-boarded with green and gold meadows that melted far off into the greens and blues of a forest. Rain still pelted down, lightning flashed in every direction, and thunder boomed and crackled. The rainstorm swept out over the valley, and high above Lavender the clouds began to split apart. The rains stopped and sunlight broke through the clouds and poured down on the valley below. Then, like the wave of a magician's wand, the most vivid rainbow she had ever seen arched across the vale, shimmering against the rain.

Then something amazing began to happen. One end of the rainbow turned a brilliant glowing gold. As Lavender watched, the golden color moved up and across the arch until the whole rainbow was covered with gold, as though God had painted it himself with the touch of his hand!

Lavender stared and stared. She had never in her life seen anything so beautiful as that golden rainbow shining like a beacon in the dark, stormy sky.

In one great leap, the Unicorn jumped off the rock and galloped down the steep slope. He sprinted across open meadows, leaped over rock walls and dodged through gaps in the hedges. As they rode, Lavender saw that the golden rainbow didn't stay in the distance like the ordinary rainbow she had seen after school. Instead, she and the Unicorn seemed to be coming closer and closer to it.

Now she saw the forest ahead. The rainbow towered above the treetops, and its end seemed to come down just where a little brook emerged from the trees. The Unicorn galloped straight for the brook, and Lavender saw that a path ran beside it into the woods. As they came under the trees, she lost sight of the rainbow. The next minute, to her surprise, she was surrounded by cheering faeries. Everywhere Lavender looked, woodland faeries were sitting in the trees and on rocks along the path, clapping and cheering for her as she passed.

Soon they reached a meadow where a moss-covered rock wall ran beside the brook. The Unicorn halted, so quickly and gently that Lavender wasn't even shaken in her seat. Directly in front of them stood a green hillside with windows and doors and a path leading up to it. Part of the hill was covered in blossoming wisteria vines and other brightly colored flowers. The end of the glowing golden rainbow came right down upon the hilltop. The meadow around the hill was filled with roses, snapdragons, sunflowers and fluttering butterflies. Birds were singing as they flew in and out of the golden rainbow.

Lavender saw that all around her were hundreds of magical creatures. Unicorns, forest pixies, trolls, leprechauns, elves, fauns, centaurs—just about every magical creature Lavender had ever heard of had come to see her reach the end of the golden rainbow. She saw Mr. McDarby smiling up at her as he came to lead her and the Unicorn toward the rock wall. Lavender looked to the other side, and here was the Pooka in goblin form, all smiles and waving at her. The water nymph was sitting on his shoulder. Behind both of them came the Banshee and all the gnomes from the castle.

Then Lavender understood that they must have been part of Wisteria's tests all along. She smiled and waved at all of them with gratitude.

The beauty and wonder around her moved her heart in a way that was beyond description. She pressed on toward the path, eagerly looking for Wisteria, whom she could not wait to meet. When a figure emerged from the door of the hill and walked down the path, all the cheering faeries instantly fell silent to watch her.

Lavender could see that Wisteria was stunning but also very humble looking. This was a Queen who chose a small country hill dwelling over a mighty castle. Her hair was intertwined with flowers and leaves, and her simple dress flowed in the gentle breeze, earthy yet elegant. Her eyes were beautiful, yet filled with wisdom and kindness.

As Wisteria approached, Lavender jumped down from the Unicorn's back. She had reached the mystical place where light and water collide and create the rainbow, a place no other human had ever reached. And this was a magical rainbow seen only once before, and reserved for the purest of hearts.

In the golden light, Wisteria came smiling to meet her and wrapped her in a warm embrace. Lavender instantly noticed how soft Wisteria's skin was and how she smelled just like the wisteria flowers in her front yard. With those soft, safe arms around her, Lavender choked up, remembering all she had gone through for Rose. Now here she was being held by a great and powerful faerie Queen, and she knew that Rose had been saved, and everything was going to be fine. Then Wisteria held Lavender away and looked her in the eyes.

"Hello, my dear Lavender Blue, it's an honor and a delight to finally meet you," said Wisteria.

"It's more of an honor to meet you, Wisteria. I have heard quite a bit about you from Professor Priddle's book. You don't look at all to be ten thousand years old," said Lavender.

"Why, thank you, Lavender," Wisteria laughed. "It's good to hear that my book is in good hands, though most people who come across it don't believe a word of it anyway. Please come in, we have a lot to talk about."

As they walked up the path, Lavender realized that parts of the meadow were actually in the rainbow, and that she was walking right through it. She could feel a tingling, warm sensation all through her body. Wisteria opened the door for Lavender and they walked inside.

Inside and out, the hill dwelling was not at all what Lavender had imagined. The elegant castle of the ball had come right out of Lavender's visions of what a faerie queen's home would be like. She liked the hill home much better than the castle. She felt completely comfortable here, and she saw that Wisteria was not at all pretentious, but humble and down to earth.

In Wisteria's living room, a fire burned in an old stone fireplace. Antique plates and an old clock sat on the mantel, and the walls and ceiling were textured white with wood beams. There was an old wooden desk and numerous book shelves filled with many old books, and vases full of flowers and herbs all around. The wooden chairs were plumped with soft cushions, and a low table held a tray with two delicate china teacups and a china teapot all ready to pour out. The beautiful light of the rainbow came in at the windows, where green trees and flowers could be seen outside. It was the kind of home Lavender hoped to have when she was grown up.

They walked outside into the backyard garden where Wisteria poured tea for both of them. "You probably have a million questions, Lavender, so ask away," said Wisteria, taking a sip of tea.

"Oh, Wisteria, I do have a million questions, but mostly I just want to thank you for saving Rose."

"It was you who saved Rose, not I. Only the love of a human can save another human. Had you not wished to take Rose's place, then my magic would have failed."

"But you still knew how to heal her. How do you have such great wisdom, Wisteria? How is it that you see so much?"

"All that I know I learned over many years, as all the answers are hidden like a puzzle inside the framework of nature," said Wisteria. "Faeries use magic to unlock these mysteries, but humans can do the same thing, only you call it Science, not Magic. In the long run, science will always outdo faerie magic. Your Wizards and wise men and women are your scientists. They deserve the highest respect, for it is reason that unlocks the mysteries of the universe."

Lavender giggled, thinking of Professor Priddle as a great Wizard. "I guess I better start listening more in class if I want to be a great wizard!"

"I think you would make a very powerful and wise Wizard," said Wisteria seriously. "You could shed light upon the world in so many ways, but most importantly because you would use your knowledge for good!"

Lavender took another sip of tea then looked up at Wisteria again. "While I could probably think of a hundred more questions, I guess I just have one more that I need to ask you. What is the meaning of the rainbow?"

"That's a wonderful question! The answer is not an easy one." Wisteria paused and thought for a moment. "Billions of years ago when the earth was very young,

oceans began to cover the land, and for the first time, clouds grew large enough to rain. You can imagine how that very first rainbow might have looked, shimmering long before there were animals or plants or anything living. From then on, every living thing, from the earliest life forms to dinosaurs to the oldest faeries and humans, has endured rain and storms, only to see a majestic rainbow shimmering like an arch of hope in a dark, stormy sky. We all experience storms in life. Just remember that there is a light in the depth of your darkness and calm at the eye of every great storm. That is where the wisdom is. Inside ourselves is often where we can find that light."

Lavender sat in silence for several minutes, thinking of all she had learned and experienced on her journey. How bleak things had looked when she thought she would never save Rose, and yet all along the darkness had a plan and a purpose.

Out front, the faeries began to chant Lavender's name.

"They want to see their hero one more time," Wisteria said. "You showed them there could be a

golden rainbow and hope for a better tomorrow, even in the human realm." Wisteria rose to her feet. "And it's time for you to go, Lavender."

"Do you think I can come back and visit again sometime? Could I maybe bring Rose? Maybe visit Mr. McDarby and the Pooka and everyone else?"

"I am afraid not," said Wisteria. "You were brought into the faerie realm only to be tested, and you must return to the human realm. You must promise not to tell anyone about any of this. We will always be here watching you, but our paths will only cross again if powers greater than mine decide so."

"I can't tell anyone?" asked Lavender wistfully.

"Well, I suppose you can tell Professor Priddle," Wisteria said with a smile. "No one will believe him anyway."

"I will always remember you and all the other faeries and all you have done for me! Thank you, Wisteria! Thank you so much for giving me back my friend Rose!" said Lavender. Tears were running down her cheeks as they walked back inside toward the front door.

Wisteria opened the gate, and all the faeries began to cheer again as they walked outside. The Unicorn was

waiting to take Lavender home, and Mr. McDarby gave her a boost to jump on his back. Lavender looked back one last time. Wisteria smiled and waved at her. Lavender looked around at all the other faeries and saw all those who had tested her, even the Banshee, and all those who had followed and stayed with her even into the Banshee's wood. She waved to them all, then in an instant the Unicorn was off and running through the forest.

For the first few miles, there were faeries along the trail, waving as Lavender rode by. Slowly she began to feel herself slipping into a dreamy state of mind, and her surroundings blurred. Then there was a bright flash, and Lavender found herself walking through a field of wildflowers. She looked around in surprise. The Unicorn was gone, and so was the forest. This was the path she always took to Rose's house, and the house was just ahead.

Lavender remembered the necklace, and reached into the pouch of iron dust to see if it was still there. Instead, she found a blossoming rose, the same rosebud she had taken to bed the night she made her wish. Suddenly, she heard a voice calling her name. She looked up, and there was Rose running toward her, more beautiful and healthy than she had ever looked before.

"Lavender! Lavender!" Rose called out. "I am all better!"

Lavender ran toward Rose with tears pouring down her cheeks. Even though Wisteria had told her that Rose was healed, only now that Rose was in front of her did it become real. They reached one another and flew together in a heartfelt hug.

Lavender was crying so hard she could barely talk. "I was so afraid for you, Rose. I thought I was going to lose you. I don't ever want to lose you!" She pulled back to look at Rose again.

"Last night around dark, I suddenly started to feel better and better," Rose said breathlessly. "Then by midnight I felt better than I have ever felt! It must be a miracle! The doctor says I am completely well."

For the rest of the day Rose and Lavender walked and visited, enjoying one another's company and friendship. Lavender simply wanted to take in the moment and be grateful her dearest friend was all better.

As Wisteria wished, Lavender would never tell Rose about her journey with the faeries of Galtee Wood, but she told Professor Priddle all about it. He was so overwhelmed with Lavender's story that he wrote down every word she told him, and kept the story safely in his faerie book until the day he died.

From that day forward, Lavender spent all her extra time learning about science and nature and the universe. She had learned from Wisteria that her own dream was to become a great wizard of science and to change the world for the better. From time to time she would take walks with Rose through the Galtee Woods, always keeping an eye out for leprechauns, pixies and water nymphs.

Though she never seemed to see them, she knew with every step that they were there. Perhaps a little fellow was hiding behind a rock or sitting in a tree, watching and laughing, and remembering that she was that special human who brought a golden rainbow over the magical woods. She was the girl with the golden heart.

Finis

SOME REAL IRISH PLACES FOUND IN LAVENDER BLUE

On a visit to Ireland the author, Steve Richardson was moved by Ballysaggartmore Towers (opposite left) which inspired the castle ruin scene in Lavender Blue, with the twisted gnomes. The real Galtee Woods in Ireland's Galtee Mountains surrounded by the Golden Vale (opposite lower left) were also very inspirational to Richardson.

The lower image on this page is of the real Glen of Aherlow with Galtee Woods and Mountains beyond the glen.

The wonderful owners of Ballinacourty House Bed and Breakfast, Glen of Aherlow, Co. Tipperary, told the author of an Irish wishing site known as St. Berrihert's Kyle, with both Celtic and Christian markings. (opposite upper right) It's found off the beaten path deep in the Galtee Woods and if visiting the area you would need good directions from the locals to find it. Originally it was just a circular enclosure, much overgrown with no buildings visible. It dates from 7th to 9th centuries. Steve describes the experience of visiting the area as "Haunting and full of Irish faerie magic!"

Lismore Castle (opposite, lower right), in Waterford Ireland, just south of the Galtee Woods was another inspirational place for the author and impacted ideas for the book.

All photos taken by the author except his portrait taken by Danial Tipton.

Lavender

Acknowledgements

I would like to acknowledge the following people for their contributions to this book: Most importantly my brother John Albert Richardson, Dec. 6th 1967 - Oct. 9th 1982 and nephews Kendall Laurence Jameson, November 25, 1987 - June 26, 1988 and Evan James Martinez, Nov. 19th 1994 - Sept. 3rd 2000. The loss of those children and the dark emotions from those times were the primary force in inspiring this book.

I would also like to thank Larry MacDougall for the illustrations and sketches, capturing the essence of the story to perfection. Karen Hayes for her brilliant critiques and editing as the book simply would not have been anywhere close to the final product without her help. Thomas Haller Buchanan for his brilliant art direction and graphic design, taking the visual quality of Lavender Blue to a level that is rarely reached in publishing these days. Matt Tegmeyer for giving the book a better direction early on. Herb Leonhard for his contributions to the graphic design and getting the book ready for the printer. The following people also influenced the book in one way or another and I would like to thank them as well: Chris and Mary Tegmeyer, Aubrey Holloway, Elizabeth Loman, Anna Kohulka, and the Las Cruces Page Turners.

Steve Richardson